Bunny's Garden

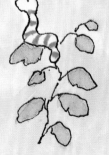

Bear and Bunny

Library of Congress Cataloging-in-Publication Data. Koscielniak, Bruce. Bear and Bunny grow tomatoes / by Bruce Koscielniak.   p.   cm. — (Umbrella books)   Summary: A hard-working bear and a lazy bunny both plant tomatoes in their gardens, with quite different results. ISBN 0-679-83687-X (trade) ISBN 0-679-93687-4 (lib. bdg.) |1. Gardening—Fiction. 2. Bears—Fiction. 3. Rabbits—Fiction.| I. Title. II. Series. PZ7.K8523Be 1993 |E|—dc20 92-10065

Grow Tomatoes

by BRUCE KOSCIELNIAK

AN UMBRELLA BOOK

Alfred A. Knopf • New York

AN UMBRELLA BOOK PUBLISHED BY ALFRED A. KNOPF, INC.

One winter, Bear decided to grow tomatoes.

And so did Bunny.

In spring, Bear began by digging a place for his tomato garden.

Bunny didn't want to waste time preparing anything. He poured his packet of seeds on the hard, weedy ground.

Bear took care to rake all the clumps, stones, and weeds out of his soil.

Bunny put up a sign and went for a folding chair.

Bear worked hard pulling out all the weeds and hauling away all the stones from his garden.

Bunny made lemonade in his blender and found a favorite book. Then he got a big pillow and went out to watch his garden grow.

Bear made small seed holes and dropped a
few seeds into each one.

Bunny dropped some lemon seeds.

Soon, little green sprouts were popping up
in Bear's garden.

Bunny couldn't be sure *what* was growing
in his garden.

Bear put in tomato sticks to help his tomatoes
grow tall and straight.

Bunny put in a swimming pool and invited
Bear to his pool party.
"Maybe some other time," said Bear. "I'm
busy right now."

A gentle summer rain fell as Bear went out to weed his garden. Now the tomato plants were almost to the tops of the sticks.

In Bunny's garden, the weeds had grown almost to the tops of his windows.

At night, Bear slept lightly so he would be able
to hear anyone who might wander uninvited
into his garden.

"Who's there?" he would growl.

Bunny slept like a ball of yarn.

By August, Bear's plants were bursting with large, juicy tomatoes.

"I know my tomatoes are here somewhere," muttered Bunny.

Bear ran out of boxes and baskets to put his tomatoes in.

"Now, what will I do with all these tomatoes?" he wondered.

Bear took two boxes and made his way to
Bunny's yard.

"I know you've been growing tomatoes, too,"
said Bear, "but I would like to give you these.
Maybe you can use a few extra."

"Thank you," said Bunny. "I do have a
tomato garden. I just can't find it. But when I
do, the tomatoes are sure to be colossal."

Bear had a very good harvest of tomatoes.
And so did Bunny.